Fire Engine Evan

Adapted by Jenny Miglis
Based on a teleplay by John Semper, Jr.

PSS!
PRICE STERN SLOAN

Characters created by David and Deborah Michel.

© 2002 Jay Jay the Jet Plane Productions, Inc. and KidQuest, Inc. d/b/a WonderWings.com Entertainment.
All Rights Reserved. Jay Jay The Jet Plane, Jay Jay, Revvin' Evan, Snuffy, Tracy, Herky,
Brenda Blue, and Tarrytown Airport are trademarks of KidQuest, Inc. d/b/a WonderWings.com
Entertainment. Published by Price Stern Sloan, a division of Penguin Putnam Books for Young Readers,
345 Hudson Street, New York, NY 10014. PSS! is a registered trademark of Penguin Putnam Inc.
Printed in U.S.A.

ISBN 0-8431-4575-7   A B C D E F G H I J

One sunny morning, Revvin' Evan raced to Tarrytown Airport with his siren blaring.

"What's all the racket about?" Jay Jay asked.

"I'm very excited!" cried Evan. You're looking at the new Tarrytown fire engine!"

"Wow, I bet being a fire engine is a big job," said Snuffy. "Um . . . what exactly does a fire engine do?"

Revvin' Evan spun around. "Imagine there's a fire . . . "

"First a fire alarm goes off," said Evan. ***"Brring! Brring! Brring!"***

"Then the fire engine radios the fire department for help. Code Red Alert!"

"Next the fire engine revs up his motor. *Vroom! Vroom!*"

"He puts on his flashing lights and turns on his siren really loud. *Whaaaaaaaa!* And then he races to the fire!"

"A fire engine has to put out the fire with water from his hose," Revvin' Evan continued. "Watch this!" He blasted a big spurt of water into the air.

"You see, a fire engine puts out fires and keeps everyone safe," Evan explained. "And I aim to be the best fire engine ever!"

"That sounds like fun!" said Snuffy. "Can I help?"
    Jay Jay, Tracy, and Herky looked at one another. "Us too!" they said.
    "Of course you can help! You can be my fire-fighting team, and
I'll be the team leader!" Evan said. "I'll train you to be the best team
in Tarrytown."

The rest of the day, Revvin' Evan trained his new fire-fighting team.

"Hup-two-three-four! Hup-two-three-four!"

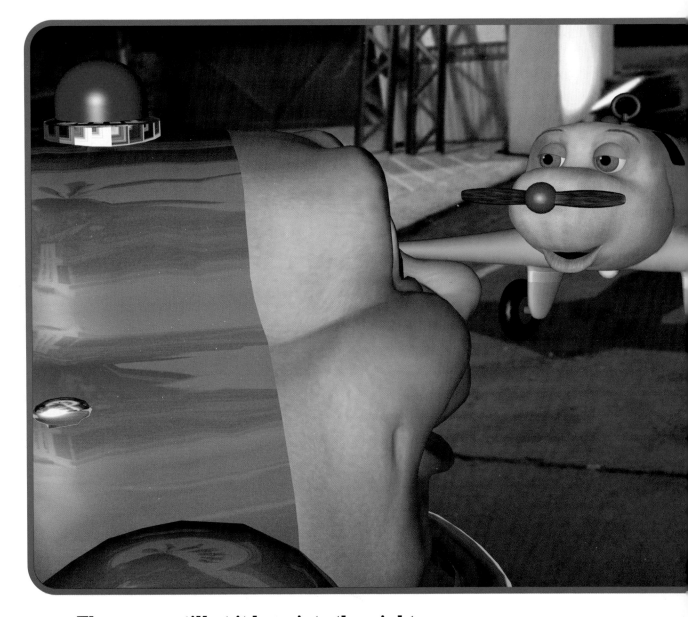

They were still at it long into the night.
"Hup-two-three-four! Hup-two-three-four! And . . . halt!"
The planes screeched to a stop.

"Well, that's a good start," Evan said. "Now for part two of the training . . . "

Jay Jay blinked hard and asked, "Um . . . what's part two?"

Evan smiled. "Bedtime!" he said. "Nighty-night, troops!"

"What a great day," Revvin' Evan said to himself. "I'm a terrific team leader."

He was heading back to the garage when he smelled something strange. He sniffed at the air. "Hmm, I think I smell smoke. And where there's smoke there's ... "

"FIRE!"

Revvin' Evan called the fire station right away. Then he
sounded the alarm and hurried to wake his fire-fighting team.
"Fire! Fire! Wake up! There's a fire!" he shouted.
But try as he might, he couldn't wake his tired team.

"I guess I'll have to put the fire out by myself," Evan said, and he sped off.

He found the fire in a trash can. It was a small fire, so he put it out quickly.

Evan called the fire station to tell them everything was okay.
"Great job, Evan!" the fireman said over the radio. "You're one
good fire engine!"

I may be a good fire engine, Evan thought, but I'm not a good team leader. He sighed. I made my team too tired to put out that little fire. If it had been a big fire we could have had big trouble.

Disappointed and very tired himself, Evan fell fast asleep.

The next morning, another fire alarm sounded in Tarrytown.
And after a good night's rest, the fire-fighting team was on the job
right away. They raced to the fire and helped put it out by remembering
all the things Revvin' Evan had taught them.

The team did such a good job that the firefighters gave them a very special thank you.

Revvin' Evan slept through it all.

Just as Evan awoke, he heard a rustling sound.

"Surprise!" the team shouted.

"Hey, what's this all about?" Evan asked.

"We helped put out a brushfire in the forest!" Snuffy said proudly.

"Oh, no!" Evan cried. "I missed it!"

"But we didn't want you to miss *this!*" Brenda Blue said, handing Evan a gold plaque. "It's the firefighters' highest award, for training the best fire-fighting team."

"Wow!" Evan exclaimed. "But next time I'll be sure I don't tire out everyone . . . or myself!"

Jay Jay smiled. "You really did turn out to be one of the best fire engines ever!"